Wishes really do come true

Lucky Stars

The Sleepover Wish

Phoebe Bright

Illustrated by Karen Donnelly

MACMILLAN CHILDREN'S BOOKS

A Working Partners book

Special thanks to Maria Faulkner

First published 2013 by Macmillan Children's Books
a division of Macmillan Publishers Limited
20 New Wharf Road, London N1 9RR
Basingstoke and Oxford
Associated companies throughout the world
www.panmacmillan.com

ISBN 978-1-4472-3654-2

Text copyright © Working Partners Limited 2013
Illustrations copyright © Karen Donnelly 2013

Created by Working Partners Limited

The right of Karen Donnelly to be identified as the
illustrator of this work has been asserted by her in
accordance with the Copyright, Designs and Patents Act 1988.

All rights reserved. No part of this publication may be
reproduced, stored in or introduced into a retrieval system, or
transmitted, in any form or by any means (electronic, mechanical,
photocopying, recording or otherwise), without the prior written
permission of the publisher. Any person who does any unauthorized
act in relation to this publication may be liable to criminal
prosecution and civil claims for damages.

1 3 5 7 9 8 6 4 2

A CIP catalogue record for this book is available from
the British Library.

Printed and bound by CPI Group (UK) Ltd, Croydon CR0 4YY

This book is sold subject to the condition that it shall not,
by way of trade or otherwise, be lent, resold, hired out,
or otherwise circulated without the publisher's prior consent
in any form of binding or cover other than that in which
it is published and without a similar condition including this
condition being imposed on the subsequent purchaser.

With thanks to all the magical people
in my life for their belief in me

Lancashire Library Services	
30118118508203	
30118125533210	
PETERS	JF
£4.99	24-Jan-2013

Contents

Contents

Hello, friend!

I'm Stella Starkeeper and I want to tell you a secret. Have you ever gazed up at the stars and thought how magical they looked? Well, you're right. Stars really do have magic!

Their precious glittering light allows me to fly down from the sky, all the way to Earth. You see, I'm always on the lookout for boys and girls who are especially kind and helpful. I train them to become Lucky Stars - people who can make wishes come true!

So the next time you're under the twinkling night sky, look out for me. I'll be floating among the stars somewhere. Do give me a wave!

Love from
Stella x

1
Lost!

It was a hot summer's day in the seaside town of Astral-on-Sea. Cassie and her best friend, Alex, were at the beach, where the sea sparkled in the warm sunlight and children splashed in the gentle waves.

Cassie was helping Alex to identify shells using a book from the library called *The Beach Explorer's Guide*.

'I think this is a cockle,' she said, holding up a pretty beige-and-white shell.

As she passed it to Alex, the charm
bracelet on her wrist jingled. Cassie looked
at the seven charms glistening brightly in
the sunshine. She smiled, remembering

how her friend Stella Starkeeper had given her the bracelet. Cassie had earned the charms by helping to make wishes come true. Each charm gave her a magical power – the bird charm allowed her to fly, and the heart gave her a perfect memory! Most special of all was the star charm, which Stella gave her when she became a Lucky Star. Now Cassie could grant wishes whenever she liked!

She looked over at Alex, who was busy inspecting the shell. He was the only other person who knew about her magical charm bracelet.

'This cockle is an excellent specimen,' he said, his dark curly head bent over the book.

Nearby, Alex's fluffy
white puppy was
digging holes.

'*Yup! Yup!*' barked
Comet, scampering
over with a shell.

'I think he's trying to help,' Cassie
laughed.

'Good boy, Comet,' Alex said.

Cassie patted the wriggly puppy. She was
so glad Alex and his family had moved to
Astral-on-Sea for good. They first became
friends last summer when Alex had stayed at
her parents' cliff-top bed and breakfast.

'Well, I must get on with my training,'
she said, putting her blonde hair in two
bunches. 'The swimming gala is only two

days away and I'd better practise if I want a chance of winning a race.'

She took off her shorts and pulled her T-shirt over her head, making the bracelet jingle again. She wondered what to do.

I don't really want to swim with my bracelet on, she thought. *What if it slips off in the sea?*

'Alex, would you look after my charm bracelet while I go for a swim?' she asked her friend.

'Yes, of course,' he replied. 'I know how special your bracelet is.'

Cassie placed the bracelet carefully in the pocket of her beach bag.

'Thanks, Alex,' she said, and ran down to the area roped off for the swimming gala. Bright orange floats bounced around in the water as some of the little children practised swimming.

Cassie waved to her friend Danny, whose black hair glistened with water as he swam along.

'Out of the way!' a screechy voice shouted.

Oh no, Cassie thought. *It's Donna Fox.*

Donna swam past Danny, splashing water everywhere. Spluttering, he blinked the water out of his brown eyes.

The Sleepover Wish

'Make way for the best swimmer in Astral-on-Sea!' she cried.

Donna stood up and pulled off her swimming hat.

'Do you like my new swimming costume?' she asked Cassie. 'It's just like the ones swimmers wear in the big races on TV. Mum said I've got to have the best!'

Cassie sighed. Donna's parents owned Flashley Manor, the most expensive hotel in Astral-on-Sea, and Donna was always showing off about her new things.

'I'm going to win the swimming gala,' Donna sneered, flicking her long hair. 'And I'll do whatever it takes.'

Cassie watched Donna march off up the beach.

'Ignore her,' Danny said to Cassie. 'Come on, let's swim together.'

For a while, Cassie swam happily with Danny. Then all of a sudden she felt a jolt go through her. It was kind of like the tingling feeling she got when she used her magic charms, but this didn't make her excited. It made her very worried. Then she felt her wrist go cold.

My bracelet! she thought. *Has something happened to it?*

Cassie called goodbye to Danny and

swam quickly to the shoreline. She ran
up the beach to where Alex was calmly
identifying shells with his magnifying glass.

'Look at these beautiful
mussels,' he said,
holding out the empty
shells with their
glistening blue surface,
but Cassie searched inside
the pocket of her bag
instead. The bracelet was
not where she had put it.

'Alex,' she said
nervously, 'did you
move my bracelet?'

'Er, no,' Alex replied. 'Why would I do
that?'

13

Cassie pointed to her bag. 'It's gone,' she said.

'Gone?' Alex gasped, looking at her. 'But it was right there. Are you sure?'

Carefully, Cassie emptied everything out of the bag. The bracelet wasn't there. She blinked back tears.

'Don't worry, we'll find it,' said Alex, searching among his shells. 'We've got to!'

Cassie checked the rug while Alex looked in the sand around it. But her bracelet wasn't anywhere to be found.

'I – I'm so sorry, Cassie,' Alex stammered. 'I was so busy looking at shells that I forgot about your bracelet . . .'

'What am I going to do?' asked Cassie anxiously.

Comet whimpered and licked her hand.

Alex thought for a moment. 'Bert came by with his donkeys while you were swimming,' he said. 'Let's ask him if he found anything.'

'Good idea,' Cassie agreed.

They sprinted down the beach to where Bert was walking the donkeys. His brown face crinkled into a smile, but when Cassie told him about the bracelet he just shook his head.

'You could ask Kara,' he said. 'She's sunbathing just over there.'

Cassie and Alex ran to where a woman

with spiky pink hair was lying on the
beach.

'No, I'm sorry. I haven't seen a charm
bracelet,' said Kara.

Head down, Cassie walked back to the
rug.

'Perhaps Comet buried it by mistake,'
said Alex. 'You could ask him.'

Cassie shook her head. 'I can't,' she said.
'I need my crescent-moon charm to talk to
animals.'

Alex looked thoughtful. 'Do you
remember in Whimsy Wood when you
used your cupcake charm to make us
invisible?'

Cassie nodded.

'And then you used your flower charm to

make something appear?' said Alex.

Cassie nodded again.

'Well, you couldn't actually see the charm bracelet then,' Alex explained. 'But the magic still worked.'

Cassie's heart lifted a little. Maybe she didn't need the bracelet to use its magic. She concentrated hard on the crescent-moon charm and

waited. Nothing happened. No familiar tingling or shower of glittery stars.

Comet yupped quietly.

18

'What's he saying?' asked Alex.

'I don't know,' Cassie replied sadly. 'I can't understand him. Now I've lost my bracelet, my magical powers have gone too!'

2
A Surprise Guest

Her lip trembling, Cassie looked around
at the beach crowded with people.
Grown-ups snoozed in the warmth of the
day and children ran by carrying buckets
full of sand. It was a perfect day, but not
for Cassie.

Where's my bracelet? she thought. *And how
will I get it back?*

Suddenly, Alex shouted, 'Cassie! Look,
what's that?'

Cassie's heart leaped. Could it be ...?
Alex was pointing to something glinting in
the sand. Very carefully she picked up the
shiny object. In her hand lay the purple star
charm from her bracelet.

'Only one charm,'
Cassie said.

'At least you've
got that,' Alex said.
'It's a start.'

Cassie put the
little charm into the pocket of her bag and
zipped it up. 'What about the other charms?
I can't make wishes come true without
them,' she said crossly.

'I'm sorry,' Alex whispered. 'I should
have looked after your bracelet better.'

22

Cassie pulled her T-shirt and shorts over
her swimsuit. The lump in her throat
stopped her speaking to him. Picking up
her bag, she turned away from Alex and
hurried home, wiping tears from her eyes.

★

That night, Cassie sat on her bed with
Twinkle, her old cat, purring in her lap.
She stroked his soft fur and looked up
through the domed glass panel of her
bedroom ceiling. In fact, Starwatcher

The Sleepover Wish

Towers had two domed observatories
for viewing the sky. Cassie's dad was
an astronomer, and he studied the stars
and planets from the bigger dome, while
Cassie's bedroom was in the smaller one.

As she gazed at the glittering stars, Cassie
thought about Stella Starkeeper, her magical
friend who lived in the Starry Sky. She
touched the little star charm, which she'd
hung on a silver necklace to keep safe.

'Stella will be so disappointed that I lost
the bracelet she gave me,' Cassie said sadly.
'And she won't be pleased about the way I
snapped at Alex either. She said the reason
she chose me to be a Lucky Star is because
I like helping. But I didn't help anybody by
getting cross.'

She hugged Twinkle.
'Oh, how I
want to be a
Lucky Star again
and grant
wishes,' said
Cassie. 'Do
you think I could
earn a new bracelet, Twinkle?'

Twinkle twitched his ears.

Just then, there was a soft knock on the
bedroom door.

'Cassie, darling, can I come in?' her mum
called. 'There's someone who really wants
to see you.'

Who could that be? Cassie thought,
carefully putting Twinkle on her starry

bedcover. And then she guessed.

Her mum opened the door and ushered Alex in ahead of her. He had his arms behind his back and was staring hard at the floor and scuffing it with the toe of his shoe. Cassie could see he was worried.

Her mum said, 'Well, I'll leave you two to chat.'

As she went back downstairs, Alex looked shyly at Cassie, his arms still tucked behind his back.

'I'm so sorry, Alex,' Cassie began to say.

But Alex interrupted, his words rushing out. 'I know it's late but I begged Mum and Dad to bring me over. Here,' he said, handing her something that he'd been hiding behind his back. 'This is for you.'

It was a homemade card. Cassie could feel a bump underneath. She turned it over and saw a green metal plate covered in colourful wires.

Alex smiled shyly. 'That's a circuit board. It took me all afternoon to make it,' he said.

'Look, it makes the card light up.'

Cassie smiled. Trust Alex to make a card with special effects. She opened it and the word 'SORRY' flashed brightly. Alex had written, 'I'm so sorry that your bracelet got lost because of me. Please let me help you find it.'

3
The Starry Sky

Cassie flung her arms round Alex and gave him a huge hug. 'Thank you so much! But I'm the one who should be saying sorry. I wasn't very nice at the beach.'

Alex beamed. 'I'm just glad we're still friends.'

'Of course we are!' said Cassie.

'Good,' said Alex. 'Now we need to work out how to find your bracelet. We just need some lateral thinking.'

'What kind of thinking?' asked Cassie, confused.

'Lateral thinking,' Alex replied. 'It means thinking of ideas that are a bit unusual.'

'We should be good at that,' said Cassie with a smile. It was great to have her best friend here to help her.

Alex sat on her bed and polished his glasses with his shirt. 'Remind me,' he said, 'what power does your star charm give you?'

Cassie touched the little star charm on her necklace. 'I got it when I became a Lucky Star. Stella gave it to me herself after I earned all the other charms.'

'That sounds pretty powerful,' Alex said, putting his glasses back on. 'Maybe this charm has some powers without the bracelet.'

'Well, the first magical thing I ever did

33

was fly,' said Cassie. 'That was after I got my bird charm.'

'Why don't you try it,' Alex suggested.

'You mean, try to fly?' said Cassie. 'If it works, I could find Stella and tell her what's happened.'

'And she might know what to do,' Alex added.

Cassie closed her eyes and concentrated hard on the star charm. At first nothing happened, but then she felt a tiny tingling in her hand.

'It's working!' Alex shouted.

Cassie opened her eyes. She was hovering above her bed.

'Wheeee!' Cassie said, twirling around the room. 'Alex, I'm going to see Stella

The Sleepover Wish

now and tell her everything.'

'Good luck,' said Alex. He pulled on the lever that opened the domed window.

'Thanks,' Cassie replied. 'See you tomorrow!' She looked upward. Then, with a *whoosh*, she soared into the Starry Sky.

Cassie flew higher and higher until the lights of Astral-on-Sea twinkled far below. It felt good to be flying again! All around her, violet and gold stars danced in the velvety darkness.

But where's Stella? wondered Cassie, searching for the star that glowed brightest of all.

On and on she flew until she spotted Stella sitting on a softly glowing pink star. But Stella did not look like herself tonight. Her shiny jacket was dull, and a star-shaped button on the cuff was hanging loose. Her short silky dress, glittering leggings and shiny boots had lost their sparkle, and her face looked pale.

Shocked, Cassie flew over and sat next to her friend.

'Hello, Cassie,' Stella said with a sad smile.

'Oh, Stella, what's wrong?' Cassie asked, giving her friend a hug.

'My powers are
fading, but I don't
know why . . .'
Suddenly, Stella gasped
and stared at Cassie's
wrist. 'Your bracelet's
gone!'

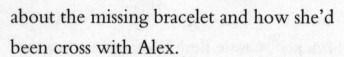

With a sinking
heart, Cassie
explained to Stella
about the missing bracelet and how she'd
been cross with Alex.

Stella put her arm round Cassie. She
sighed. 'Everyone makes mistakes. And now
I know why my powers are fading.'

'Why?' Cassie asked.

'When a Lucky Star is separated from

his or her charm bracelet, the power of
the Starry Sky is affected. If the magic
disappears completely, then Lucky Stars
won't be able to grant wishes any more,'
Stella replied.

Cassie was horrified. 'I'm so sorry,' she
said. 'How can I help?'

Stella smiled and gave Cassie a hug. 'If
you find your bracelet, my magical powers
will return!'

Cassie's heart sank. 'But how can I find
it? I don't know where to begin!'

4
Special Puppy Power

'A Lucky Star helps other people,' Stella said, 'but this time *you'll* need to ask for help. There are Lucky Stars in every town, city and village, all over the world,' she explained. 'Boys and girls just like you, Cassie.'

'Really?' Cassie gasped.

She sat next to Stella on the little pink star and gazed below her. She imagined Lucky Stars everywhere, granting wishes.

'To get your bracelet back,' Stella continued, 'you need to find two more Lucky Stars who will use their powers to help you.'

'How will I know who they are?' asked Cassie. 'Do all Lucky Stars wear bracelets just like mine?'

'Yes,' said Stella. 'But you can't just walk up to Lucky Stars and ask for help. They can't use their magic to help another Lucky Star unless you first make their wish come true.'

'But how can I make wishes come true when I don't have any magical powers of my own?' said Cassie.

'Remember when you granted Alex's wish?' Stella asked her.

Cassie nodded. Alex had wished for a best friend, and Cassie herself had been the answer to his dream.

'You made Alex's wish come true without any magic at all – just imagination and determination,' Stella went on.

'I did,' Cassie agreed, her hopes rising. 'But how will I know where to look for other Lucky Stars?'

Stella pointed to Cassie's star charm. 'This is a very special charm. It gives you the magic from your first charm, the power to fly. But the star charm will also have a power of its own.'

'What power is that?' asked Cassie.

'That's up to you to decide,' Stella told her. 'But choose wisely, as you will only have your star charm to help you find your bracelet.'

'I will,' Cassie promised.

She kissed Stella goodbye and flew home.
Dropping through her bedroom window,
she closed the glass panel and snuggled
into bed with Twinkle. Her fingers closed
around the little star charm.

I wonder what power I should choose, she
thought sleepily. *And I can't wait to meet
more Lucky Stars . . .*

The next morning, Cassie and Alex were
sitting in the kitchen of Starwatcher
Towers.

'Mum and Dad are going on a trip for
Mum's work,' said Alex, 'so they've
asked your parents if I can stay here for
two nights. It'll be just like when I was

staying at your B & B on holiday.'

'Brilliant!' said Cassie. 'Let's make it a proper sleepover, with a midnight feast and everything! Can we?' she asked her parents. 'Please?'

Cassie saw her mum and dad grin at each other.

'We had the same idea,' said her mum, glancing up from her laptop, where she was checking the B & B bookings.

'Really?' said Cassie. 'That's brilliant!'

'What do you think this is for?' said her dad, as he opened the oven door to check on the cake he was baking.

'That smells absolutely yummy,' Cassie said.

Alex nodded. 'The delicious smell comes from heating the sugar and other ingredients.'

Cassie smiled. Only Alex would know the scientific reason for the smell of baking!

I'm glad Alex and I are still best friends, she

thought. *He'll help me find two more Lucky Stars so we can get my bracelet back!*

She led Alex out into the back garden. 'We're just going to plan our sleepover,' she called to her parents.

But she wasn't sure that they had heard over the sound of her dad loading the dishwasher.

Outside, Cassie told Alex about her visit to Stella last night.

'What magical power should I choose for my star charm?' she asked him. 'It's got to be something that will help me find my bracelet.'

They both stood silently for a minute, thinking hard. At their feet, Comet gave a little whine and sniffed around a plant pot as if trying to find something.

Cassie smiled. 'I don't think there's any cake under there, Comet!' she said.

'That's it!' Alex clicked his fingers. 'Comet has an extra-strong sense of smell that helps him find things. It's like his special puppy power.'

'So I need a special power to help me find the other Lucky Stars,' Cassie added excitedly.

'Not just to find them,' Alex said. 'To *take* you to the Lucky Stars.'

Just then, Comet found a dog biscuit behind the plant pot and ate it up!

Cassie and Alex laughed.

'So that's what he smelt!' said Alex. 'You see, his puppy power took him right to the dog biscuit.'

'Clever Comet!' said Cassie. 'Let's see if I can give my charm the power to take me to a Lucky Star.'

They ran to the end of the garden, Comet trotting along at their heels.

Cassie stood next to Alex and took his hand. 'When I used my cupcake charm, I held your hand so you could be invisible too. So maybe if we hold hands now the magic will take you to the Lucky Star as well.'

Alex squeezed Cassie's hand. She closed her eyes and concentrated on her star charm.

The Sleepover Wish

Please take me to another Lucky Star . . .

She opened her eyes but nothing had happened. 'It isn't working,' she said.

Then all of a sudden the garden began to spin, becoming a great swirl of tiny sparkling stars. Cassie felt something furry against her bare leg . . .

Lucky Stars

Whoosh! The stars spun even faster and Starwatcher Towers began to fade.

Cassie's heart raced with excitement. *Where will my star charm take us?*

5
Jupiter Farm

The whirling stars cleared. Cassie and Alex
weren't in the garden any more. They
were standing near a gate that led into a
farm.

'*Yup!*'

'Oh, Comet!' Cassie smiled. 'You're the
furry thing I felt.'

'His first adventure!' Alex said, stroking
the excited puppy. He stared around. 'This
is amazing. I've read all about molecules

moving instantly from one place to another.
It's called teleportation, but I didn't think it
was scientifically possible.'

'It's magically possible,' Cassie laughed.
'Perhaps it's called star travel!'

They peered over the gate. In the
farmyard they
could see
wooden
pens
filled
with
sheep
and lambs. In
a paddock nearby, cows looked up to gaze
at them before munching at the long grass
again.

'Over there,'
Alex said,
pointing.

Cassie
turned
to look.
A bright
yellow sign
read 'Jupiter
Farm'.

Jupiter Farm

'I've heard of
this farm,' she said. 'It's near
Astral-on-Sea.'

'Jupiter is the largest planet in the solar
system,' Alex added. 'This should be a good
place to find a Lucky Star.'

A cheerful lady, with stalks of straw

caught in her hair, walked over from the
sheep pens.

'Hello, I'm Mrs
Brown! Have you come
to join the Kids' Club?'
she asked. She looked
closely at Cassie as she
handed them each
a leaflet. 'You look
familiar. Are you Daisy
Cafferty's daughter, by
any chance?'

'Yes, that's me,' said
Cassie.

The lady's face
broke into a
wide smile.

'Your mum and I are old friends, but I haven't seen her in ages. I keep meaning to pop up to Starwatcher Towers for a cuppa and a chat. Tell her Belinda Brown says hello.'

'I will. Thank you, Mrs Brown,' said Cassie.

'Well,' Mrs Brown continued, 'I won't hold you up. The Kids' Club has started already. My daughter Hannah's over at the blue barn with the others.'

Still smiling, she hurried back to the sheep pens.

Cassie read the leaflet out loud. '"*Learn how to take care of baby animals.*" That sounds like a great place to start looking. Lucky Stars love helping.'

'Let's go then,' said Alex.

Together they walked up the rough
track until they reached a
wooden barn painted
bright blue.
Outside, a
group of
children
was
gathered
around a girl
who Cassie
guessed was
about the
same age as
her and Alex.
The girl wore

muddy black boots and a sleeveless
green jacket. Her red hair was tied into a
ponytail.

'Hi,' the girl said, waving to them.
'Come and join us. My name's Hannah.'

'I'm Cassie and this is Alex,' Cassie
said.

'*Yup!*' Comet barked.

'And this is my puppy, Comet,' Alex
added.

'Welcome to Jupiter Farm,' Hannah
said. 'We're just about to go into the
barn and feed the piglets. Do you want to
come?'

'Oh, yes!' said Cassie and Alex
together.

'But perhaps I'd better leave Comet out

here,' Alex said. 'He's never seen a piglet before.'

'There's an old lead hanging up by the hay bales you can use,' Hannah explained. 'If you tie one end to that tree, Comet can wait for us outside.'

Alex did as Hannah suggested and Comet lay down, his head on his paws.

Hannah led the way into the barn, where the pigs grunted, waiting for their feed.

'These piglets are old enough for adult food now,' said Hannah, giving each child a bucket filled with vegetable chunks.

The children stroked the half-grown, curly-tailed piglets, which squealed happily as they ate. The littlest piglet scrambled up Cassie's bucket, poking his nose inside.

All the children laughed. Cassie smiled at them, wondering if one of them was another Lucky Star.

'Look,' said Alex, pointing to where a bigger boy in a brown jacket was showing a

younger boy how to fill a trough with food. 'He's very helpful. Maybe he's a Lucky Star.'

'Or it might be that girl with the red jumper,' Cassie said, nodding towards a girl who was helping one of the smaller piglets to reach the food.

'*Yup!*' Comet suddenly dashed into the barn, the lead trailing behind him.

'Oh no,' Alex said. 'The knot must have come loose.'

Comet rolled on his back. The littlest piglet trotted round him.

'*Grunt!*' A big sow snorted loudly at Comet, who jumped up with a frightened yap.

Quickly, Hannah marched across the

barn and scooped the puppy into her arms.
'It's all right,' she said, gently stroking him.
'The sow is just keeping an eye on her
piglet.'

'Oh,' Cassie gasped, nudging Alex.

Hannah's sleeve had slipped down her
arm as she'd carried Comet across the barn,

revealing a bracelet that glittered with seven tiny charms!

Cassie grinned at Alex. 'I've found my first Lucky Star,' she said. 'I wonder what her wish will be?'

6
Hannah Makes a Wish

Hannah handed Comet over to Alex with a bright smile.

'We're so sorry he got into the barn,' Cassie said.

'Don't worry,' Hannah replied, patting Comet's head. 'I'm used to looking after all kinds of animals, even excited puppies.'

Outside the barn, Alex and Cassie helped to rinse out the buckets. Feeding time was

over for the pigs, and the younger
children were leaving to help feed the
calves.

'Happy birthday,' the girl with the red
jumper called to Hannah as she ran by.

'Thank you,' Hannah replied, waving to her.

'It's your birthday! How lovely,' Cassie said. 'What are you going to do to celebrate?'

'Not much.' Hannah sighed. 'It's lambing season, so my parents are too busy to plan a party.'

'What a shame,' Alex said.

Hannah nodded. 'I really wish I could have a sleepover . . .'

Cassie grinned at Alex. Hannah had made her wish, and Cassie knew exactly how to make it come true.

'Hannah, Alex is staying at my house for a sleepover tonight,' Cassie said. 'Would you like to come too?'

'Really?' Hannah said, her eyes sparkling. 'I'd love that, but I'd have to ask my mum.'

'Of course,' said Cassie. 'Your mum told me that she and my mum are old friends.'

'That's so cool!' said Hannah. 'Then she'll probably let me come.'

'When I get home, I'll ask my mum to phone her. I could ask my friend Kate as well. We can have a proper party!' Cassie said.

Hannah clapped her hands in delight. 'That would be really fun,' she said. 'I can't wait!'

'*Yup!*' Comet joined in, chasing his tail. They all laughed.

'I'd better check
on the Kids' Club,'
Hannah said,
waving as she
hurried off. 'See
you later!'

'Time for
us to go too,'
Cassie said.

They slipped
round the back of the barn. Cassie held
Alex's hand and Comet's tail. Closing her
eyes, she concentrated hard on her star
charm again, calling on its flying power to
take them home. A great swirl of sparkling
stars spun round them.

Whoosh! Jupiter Farm began to fade . . .

★

Cassie and Alex reappeared in exactly the same spot they'd left from at the end of the garden. 'I hope Mum and Dad didn't notice we were gone so long,' Cassie said.

They ran into the kitchen, Comet trotting at their heels. Cassie stopped in surprise. Her mum was still working on her laptop and her dad was still loading the dishwasher – which was exactly how they had left them!

'That's not scientifically possible,' Alex whispered to Cassie.

'It's magic,' Cassie replied. 'When we star travel, time must stand still!'

'Hello,' Cassie's mum said. 'What have you two sorted out for your sleepover?'

The Sleepover Wish

'Is it OK if I invite two more friends?'
Cassie asked. 'I'd like to ask Kate and my
new friend, Hannah. Her mum's Belinda
Brown – she says hello.'

Her mum's eyes lit up. 'Belinda
Brown! I haven't seen her in a long
time. Do you know, we used to have

sleepovers together
when we were
your age.' She
picked up her
phone. 'I'll give
her a ring to
arrange for
Hannah to
come over.
And of course
Kate can come
as well.'

'I'm sure we can find room for a couple more,' said Cassie's dad. 'I've made plenty of cake.'

He took the finished cake out of the oven and put it on a cooling tray. It smelt even better than before!

Cassie gave her dad a thank-you hug.

Alex helped Cassie get sleeping bags and duvets from the linen cupboard, ready for the sleepover. Twinkle jumped on the pile, pawing at a duvet. Laughing, they carried it all to Cassie's room.

'Let's move my bed over so we can put all the sleeping bags in the middle of the floor,' said Cassie. 'Then we can look at the stars tonight!'

'Great idea,' Alex agreed.

Soon they had four neat rows of bedding under the glass panel in the ceiling.

Cassie's mum walked in with the pillows. 'How are you two getting on?' she asked.

'We're all ready for the sleepover!' said
Cassie with a smile.

'Now we just have to wait for tonight!'
added Alex.

The Sleepover Wish

They were both bursting with excitement.

The sleepover's going to be such fun, thought Cassie. *And when I've granted Hannah's wish, I'll ask her to help me find my bracelet and help Stella feel strong again.*

7
Starry Sleepover

That evening, Cassie and Alex waited impatiently for their guests. Kate arrived first, carrying an overnight bag that was stuffed full.

'I've brought my pyjamas, my furry slippers and my big teddy, and even my MP3 player and some mini-speakers,' she said, pulling things out of her bag.

'Brilliant!' Cassie said. 'We can dance later!' She gave a little twirl.

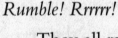

Rumble! Rrrrrr!

They all ran out of the front door to see what the noise was.

'Wow, look at that truck!' Alex said, pointing down the hill. Chugging up towards them was a huge farm truck full of bales of hay.

'It's Hannah!' Cassie said, clapping her hands excitedly.

They ran down the garden path, waving. Cassie's mum followed them out. When

Mrs Brown climbed from the truck, Cassie's mum flung her arms round her.

'It's so good to see you, Belinda,' she said. 'Come in for a cup of tea. We've got a lot to catch up on!'

Chattering away, the two mums went inside.

Further down the hill, Cassie noticed a girl making slow progress up the slope on a shiny red bicycle.

Who could this be? Cassie thought. As the girl got closer, Cassie recognized her long hair and scowling face.

'Hi, Donna,' Cassie said.

Donna skidded to a halt in front of them. She was gasping for breath and had hair stuck to her sweaty forehead.

'What d'you think of my new bike?'
Donna asked, panting.

'Er, very nice,' Alex replied.

'Nice? This bike is better than nice,'
said Donna. 'Mummy and Daddy got me
the latest model. It's the best money can
buy.'

Grinning smugly
at Cassie, she turned
the bike round.

Alex led Kate and

Hannah into

Starwatcher

Towers, but

Cassie

stayed by

the gate,

watching Donna zoom back down the hill.

That's strange, she thought. *Cycling all the way up that hill must have been very hard work, even on the best bike money can buy. I know Donna's a huge show-off, but was there another reason she came?*

A few minutes later, Cassie and her friends were all up in her bedroom listening to music on Kate's MP3 player. When they heard the pop star Jacey Day singing 'Magic Moments', Alex and Cassie showed the others their special dance routine. They had performed it onstage with Jacey at the Songs on the Sand music festival last summer.

'I made up this
move,' Alex
said,
moving
his arms
like a wave.

Laughing,
Hannah and Kate joined in.

'I think we should eat now,' Cassie said.

'Yes!' Alex agreed. 'I'm starving after all
that dancing!'

They sat down on the bedding and
tucked into the snacks that Cassie's parents
had prepared. Purring loudly, Twinkle
snuggled between Cassie and Hannah.

Cassie reached up to the shelf for a large
plate covered with a starry cloth.

'Ta-da!' she said, pulling the cover off.

It was the cake that her dad had made. Cassie and Alex had decorated it with the words 'Happy Birthday, Hannah' in bright yellow icing.

'What an amazing cake!' said Hannah. 'Thank you so much. This birthday sleepover is a wish come true!'

Cassie looked at Alex and they nodded to one another. *It's time to tell Hannah who I am*, Cassie thought.

'Kate, can you help me identify the shells I've collected?' said Alex. He led Kate to the desk where he pulled out *The Beach Explorer's Guide* and some of the seashells he had found the day before. Cassie smiled.

She knew that Alex had looked up the
shells already, but he was keeping Kate busy
so she could talk to Hannah alone.

'I like your bracelet,' Cassie told Hannah,
admiring the pretty charms.

'Thank you. It's very special,' Hannah
replied.

'I know,' Cassie said quietly.

Cassie held out her little star charm and
Hannah raised her eyebrows in surprise.

'Are you . . . ?' she said.

Cassie nodded. 'Yes,' she answered
quietly. 'I'm a Lucky Star, just like you.'

Hannah beamed and gave Cassie a
squeeze. 'I've never met another Lucky Star
before. How exciting,' she whispered.

Cassie took a deep breath. 'I *am* a Lucky

Star, but I've got a problem and I need your help.'

She told Hannah how she had lost her bracelet.

'Stella Starkeeper's powers are fading and it's all my fault,' said Cassie. 'I need to

find my bracelet to save her. If her magic disappears, then Lucky Stars won't be able to grant wishes any more.' Cassie felt a lump in her throat, but she had to tell Hannah everything. 'Stella told me that I needed to find two more Lucky Stars and make their wishes come true,' she explained. 'Then they can share their magic with me.'

'Well, you've certainly made a wish come true for one Lucky Star,' said Hannah with a smile.

The girls looked around the bedroom. Twinkle and Comet were curled up on a duvet, while Kate and Alex were eating cake as they looked at seashells.

'This sleepover's been brilliant! Thank you,' Hannah said.

'Would you help me find my bracelet?' asked Cassie. She held her breath, waiting for Hannah's answer.

Hannah smiled again. 'Of course I will!'

Cassie lay curled up in a heap of bedding on the floor, her moon-shaped bedside lamp casting a soft glow across the room. When she was sure her guests were asleep, she slipped out from under the covers

The Sleepover Wish

and opened the glass panel in her ceiling.
Taking out her star charm, she concentrated
on it very hard, until, in a shower of
sparkles, she flew up into the Starry Sky.

Lucky Stars

Stella was seated on the same little pink star. Her brilliance had faded even more. Even her wand was a dull grey now, but she smiled as Cassie flew towards her.

'Stella,' Cassie called. 'I've found my first Lucky Star.'

She told her magical friend all about Hannah and the sleepover party.

'I knew you could do it,' Stella said, a faint sparkle appearing in her eyes. 'Tomorrow you must find another Lucky Star to help you. Three Lucky Stars should be strong enough to find your bracelet.'

'Then you'll have your powers back too,' said Cassie. 'Will you be OK until then?'

Stella nodded. 'Of course. Now you must go home and enjoy your sleepover.'

The Sleepover Wish

Cassie kissed Stella goodbye and floated back across the Starry Sky towards Starwatcher Towers.

Through the glass panel of her bedroom ceiling she saw her three friends sleeping in a row. Comet was curled up by Alex's feet and Twinkle was tucked between Kate and Hannah.

Cassie lay down beside them and gave a sleepy smile. She knew that with her friends' help she'd find her bracelet soon – and then both she and Stella would have all their magical powers back. *Tomorrow I'll find another Lucky Star and help another wish come true!* she thought, before closing her eyes and falling fast asleep.

Cassie's Things to Make and Do!

Join in the Lucky Stars fun!

I hope you enjoyed my Sleepover Wish Story. There are all sorts of fun things you can do at your own sleepover party, so why not have a go!

Make Your Own Banana-and-honey Face Mask

You will need

1 banana

half a teaspoon
    of lemon
    juice

1 tablespoon of
    honey

How to make

1. Mash the banana and honey together to form a paste, then stir in the lemon juice – make sure the mixture is not too watery.

2. Smooth the paste over your face and neck.

3. Leave this on for fifteen minutes before rinsing with warm water. This will leave your skin feeling lovely and refreshed!

Decorate Pillowcases

A decorated pillowcase can make a lovely souvenir so that all the good memories from your sleepover will last forever!

You will need

One plain pillowcase per guest
(you need to have permission to
write on these)
Permanent markers or fabric pens
Glitter-glue pens
Sequins
Fabric glue

How to make

All you need to do is decorate your pillowcase in whatever style you like. Everyone can sign each other's to create a truly memorable party souvenir!

Bake Cupcakes

Cupcakes are fun to make as well as delicious to eat, so why not try baking your own?

For the cakes you will need

250g unsalted butter

250g caster sugar

250g self-raising flour

pinch of salt

4 medium eggs

4 tablespoons milk

2 x 12-hole muffin tins, lined
   with paper cases

For the icing you will need

140g butter

280g icing sugar

1–2 tablespoons milk

few drops food colouring

Cassie's Top Tip:

Try different toppings to make them extra special!

How to make the cakes

1. Preheat the oven to 190°C or gas mark 5.

2. Beat the butter in a large bowl until soft. Add the sugar, flour, salt, eggs and milk, and whisk until the mixture is smooth.

3. Use a spoon to divide the mixture between all the paper cases.

4. Place both muffin tins in the oven and bake for fifteen minutes until the cupcakes are a light golden colour.

5. Remove the tins from the oven using oven gloves – it may be best to ask an adult to help you.

6. Leave the cupcakes to cool in the tins for a few minutes, and then transfer them to a wire rack.

7. Decorate with buttercream icing (see opposite).

How to make the buttercream icing

1. Beat the butter in a large bowl until soft. Add half the icing sugar and beat until smooth.

2. Add the remaining icing sugar and one tablespoon of the milk and beat the mixture until creamy and smooth. Beat in the rest of the milk, if necessary, to loosen the mixture.

3. Stir in the food colouring until the buttercream is the colour you want.

Perfect for a midnight feast!

Do Your Hair Up in Rag Curls

On your sleepover, have fun and create
cute curls by tying them
with rags to make
gorgeous wavy
locks, like Stella
Starkeeper! This
works on all
lengths of hair.

How to do

★ Wash your hair, then use leave-in
conditioner and comb it through your
hair thoroughly. This will work best on
quite wet hair.

★ Tear an old sheet or other soft cloth into strips.

★ Part your hair down the middle and tie one side in a ponytail.

★ Take a strip of cloth and roll a section of hair from the other side of your head around it from bottom to top until you reach your scalp.

★ Tie the loose ends of the rag on top of the curl in a single knot to keep it in place.

★ Repeat this method with the rest of your hair.

★ In the morning, take out the rags. You will then have a beautiful head of curls to style however you like.

While Cassie was training to be a Lucky Star, she made lots of new friends. You'll meet them all too in the Lucky Stars stories!

Cassie

Alex

Comet

Twinkle

Stella

Hannah

Kate

Donna

Cassie's mum

Cassie's dad

Wishes really do come true

Lucky Stars

The Best Friend Wish

Phoebe Bright

With a whizz, fizz
and pop, magical Stella
Starkeeper appears and tells
Cassie she will be a Lucky Star –
someone who can grant wishes.
Could Alex, her new friend,
have a secret wish?

Wishes really do come true

Lucky Stars

The Perfect Pony Wish

Phoebe Bright

Sunbeam the pony has
run away! Cassie must help
a little girl's wish come true and
find him before the showjumping
competition begins. Will
Sunbeam be the perfect pony?

Wishes really do come true
Lucky Stars

Explore the magical world of Lucky Stars!

For fun things to make and do – as well as games and quizzes – go to:

www.luckystarsbooks.co.uk

Wishes really do come true

Lucky Stars

Cassie is training to become a Lucky Star –
someone who can make wishes come true!
Follow her on more exciting adventures as
she meets new friends in need of help.

The Best Friend Wish

The Perfect Pony Wish

The Pop Singer Wish

The Birthday Wish

The Film Star Wish

The Ballerina Wish

The Christmas Wish

www.luckystarsbooks.co.uk